LAWRENCEBURG P

For David Charles Goodhart
with love – PG
For Dad – JK

Crabtree Publishing Company
www.crabtreebooks.com

PMB 16A, 350 Fifth Avenue,
Suite 3308,
New York, NY
10118

612 Welland Avenue,
St. Catharines,
Ontario, Canada
L2M 5V6

Published by Crabtree Publishing Company in 2004
Published in 2002 by Random House Children's Books and Red Fox

Cataloging-in-Publication data
Goodhart, Pippa.
  Slow magic / written by Pippa Goodhart ; illustrated by John Kelly.
    p. cm. – (Flying foxes)
Summary: Polly's grandparents teach her about the magic of nature
by showing her how a seed can be transformed into something warm
to wear.
  ISBN 0-7787-1482-9 (RLB) – ISBN 0-7787-1528-0 (PB)
  [1. Nature–Fiction. 2. Grandparents–Fiction.] I. Kelly, John, 1964-
ill. II. Title. III. Series.
PZ7.G6125Sl 2004
[E]–dc22

2003022721
LC

Set in Cheltenham Book Infant

1 2 3 4 5 6 7 8 9 0 Printed and bound in Malaysia by Tien Wah Press 0 9 8 7 6 5 4 3

Slow Magic

Pippa Goodhart · John Kelly

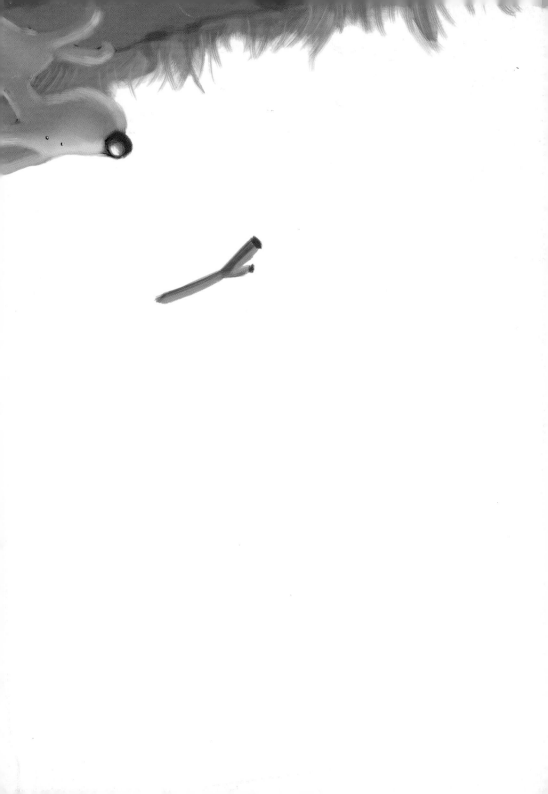

One day Grandpa asked,
"Do you want me to do
some magic?"
"Only magicians can
do magic," said Polly.

5

"And who says I'm not a magician?" said Grandpa. "See this grass? I can turn it into four different things."

"I don't believe you," said Polly.
"Watch this," said Grandpa.

"Summer tree,

winter tree,

spring flowers,

April showers."

7

"That's not magic," laughed Polly. "That's the easy, quick magic," said Grandpa. "I can do better slow magic, but that takes patience. Have you got patience, Polly?"

"Yes," said Polly. "Do
some now, Grandpa!"

"Well," said Grandpa. "I could turn those grass seeds into something to keep you warm."

"Go on, then," said Polly.

"Ah," said Grandpa. "This is slow magic. We can't start the magic until next spring."

"That's ages!" said Polly. "I want to see it now!"

Grandpa laughed. "Slow magic takes patience. But if you keep those seeds safe and dry, they'll be ready to start the magic when the time comes."

All winter long, Polly kept the seeds safe and dry in a jam jar.

"When will winter be over and spring come?" she asked Grandpa, and Grandpa told her, "When you see Granny's crocus flowers coming up, you'll know that spring is here."

Polly looked out of the window. All she could see on the ground was snow.

"Oh, Grandpa," sighed Polly. "This magic is so slow, it doesn't even begin!"

"It'll be worth waiting for," said Grandpa. "Wait and see."

Polly waited, and one day she saw flowers
in Granny's garden.

"Well then," said Grandpa. "It must be
time to start the magic."

Grandpa took Polly to the big field. He showed her how to dig and rake the soil so that it was loose and fine.

"Now sprinkle your seeds," said Grandpa.

So Polly did.

"What will the grass seeds do?" asked Polly.

"If you water them and wait, then they'll grow into grass. Grass is what something likes to eat," said Grandpa.

"What kind of something?"

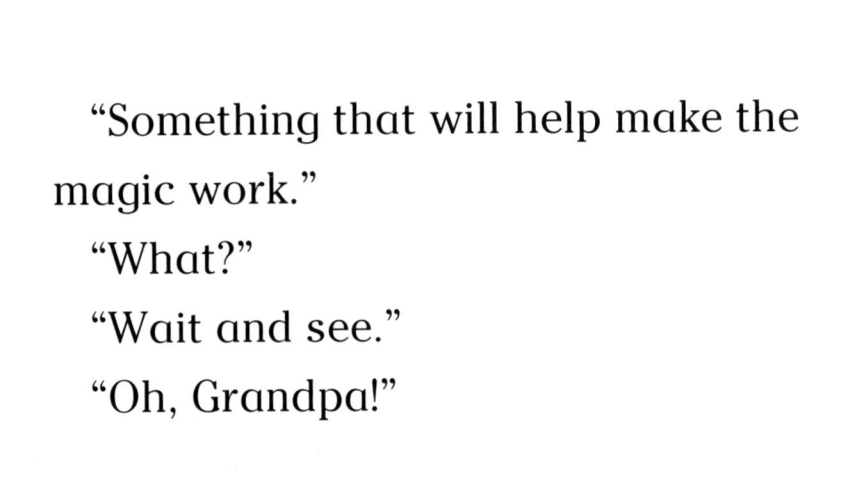

"Something that will help make the magic work."

"What?"

"Wait and see."

"Oh, Grandpa!"

Polly waited and watched for weeks.
Rain fell on the ground

and the sun shone bright and warm.

The tiny seeds opened and bright blades of grass grew. Polly bent down close and looked at her grass. She asked Grandpa, "How could such a big bit of grass come out of such a tiny little seed?"

"It's part of the magic," said Grandpa. "But there's more to come. Follow me."

Grandpa took Polly to the big barn. "These sheep have been shut inside all winter. Now that spring is here, they're hungry for some juicy fresh grass. Will you help me herd them to the field?"

Polly waved her arms and shouted
to make the sheep go into the field.

21

One sheep nibbled at Polly's patch of grass.

"Grandpa," she whispered, "that one's eating my grass!"

"Then we'll give her a special mark," said Grandpa.

"So we know for sure that she has got your grass inside her."

POLLY

22

"So my grass is turning into sheep!"
said Polly.

"It's another part of the magic," said
Grandpa. "But there's more to come.
Wait and see."

Polly waited and watched for a few more
weeks. Then her sheep gave birth to a lamb.

"It really is magic if my grass turned into
part of that lamb!"

"But there's more," said Grandpa. "Your sheep is growing something else as well as a lamb. Something on the outside."

"Wool?" guessed Polly.

"Wool," smiled Grandpa.

Spring turned into summer. The lamb grew big and Polly's sheep got hot under her wool. So Grandpa cut it off. "There," he said. "Your grass has turned into wool."

"Is that the end of the magic?" asked Polly.

"It's the end of my bit of magic," said Grandpa.

"But there's
more magic – the
kind that your granny
does best. She'll magic
you something to keep
you warm."

Polly was too hot to want
anything to keep her warm, but she
liked the idea of more magic so
she went to find Granny.

"Is your magic the slow or the fast kind?" asked Polly.

"Oh, it'll be slow, I'm afraid," said Granny. "First we must wash the wool . . . "

So Polly and Granny splash-splosh washed the heavy wet wool until it was clean and white. Then they dyed it.

"What's your favorite color, Pol?" asked Granny.

"Every color!" said Polly.
So Polly and Granny dyed the wool
purple and orange, yellow and green,

red, pink, and blue.

Then they hung it out to dry.

Autumn brought
wind and rain
outside. Granny
sat by the fire and
worked the wool
between two prickly brushes.

"Why are you doing that?" asked Polly.

"To untangle the wool and get it ready for spinning," said Granny. "You try it."

The weeks passed and Granny was busy with all sorts of things.

"Please, what's the next bit of magic?" asked Polly.

So Granny showed Polly how to twist the wool between her fingers to make a thread.

Next she spun the wool together into long long threads with a spinning wheel.

"How do short sheep hairs turn into something so long?" asked Polly.

"Just part of the magic," smiled Granny.

Then Granny began to knit the bright wool, clicking needles, row after row to make it grow.

"What is it going to be?" asked Polly.

"A sweater for you, my Pol," said Granny.

"And there's enough wool left over for you to make something too. Would you like that?"

"Yes, please!" said Polly.

So Granny showed Polly how to knit long skinny wool into something flat and warm.

"That's a kind of magic too," said Polly.

It took a long time to do.

By the time the knitting was finished, winter had come again. It was cold and a sweater was just what Polly needed.

"Grown from grass seed!" said Grandpa.

Polly had a present for Grandpa, too.
It was something to keep him warm
when he went to the fields to see
his sheep.

"Just what I need!" said Grandpa. "A nice
warm scarf made by slow magic. And which
magician made this?"

"I did!" said Polly. "And Granny and I made something for somebody else too."

"Who's that?" asked Grandpa.

"My new baby sister!" said Polly. "Can I show her the slow magic when she's big enough to be patient, Grandpa?" she asked.

"Of course," said Grandpa. "Everyone should learn how to do slow magic."

Do some slow magic of your own at home. Make a grass-head and watch it grow!

YOU WILL NEED:
an old pair of nylons, a mug, grass seeds, potting soil, string, poster paints, glue and plastic eyes

1. Cut off a foot of an old pair of nylons. Place it inside a mug and fold the edges over the sides.

2. Put a little soil at the bottom, and drop in a few grass seeds. Fill it up with potting soil, and tie up the top with string. Now turn it over so the string is at the bottom.

3. Decorate your grass-head: stick on plastic eyes and paint on the mouth. For the nose, tie up a bit of the stocking with string.

4. When the paint is dry, place your grass-head in a bowl of water so all the soil gets wet. Next, put it in a mug to drain.

Polly has to wait for spring to come to plant her seeds. The warm spring sunlight and rain showers help the seeds grow. The soil gives them food. If she planted her seeds in winter, they would freeze in the cold ground!

Can you see the seasons changing in the story? Try looking at the weather and what Polly wears. Look at the plants too.

5. Give it a drink every few days and watch it grow!

You can trim the grass hair into a funky hairdo!

Pippa Goodhart

How long did it take to write this story? First, I spent some time thinking about the story when I was peeling potatoes and lying in the bath. Then it took several days to get the words right.

Do you have a little sister like Polly? Yes, I have a little sister called Joey and I have a big brother called Dick.

Have you ever seen a lamb being born? Yes. It's a very special thing to watch. It's amazing how fast the lamb is cleaned up by its mother and gets up onto its wobbly feet after being born.

Can I be a writer like you? Yes! I wasn't quick at learning to read and I was bad at spelling and writing neatly, so I never thought I would become a writer. But I did. Good story ideas are more important than getting the writing neat. Do you play "let's pretend" games or daydream? Try turning those ideas into stories and writing them down.

What gives you good ideas? I live with my husband, Mick, and my three daughters, Annie, Mary, and Susie. We have a cat and five kittens and a pond full of fish and frogs. All my family and animals give me ideas for stories. Ideas are easy. It's shaping them into a good story that is hard!

Let your ideas take flight with

Flying Foxes

Digging for Dinosaurs
by Judy Waite and Garry Parsons

Only Tadpoles Have Tails
by Jane Clarke and Jane Gray

The Magic Backpack
by Julia Jarman and Adriano Gon

Slow Magic
by Pippa Goodhart and John Kelly

Sherman Swaps Shells
by Jane Clarke and Ant Parker

That's Not Right!
by Alan Durant and Katharine McEwen

John Kelly

Meet the illustrator.

What did you use to paint the pictures in this book? The drawings were all done the old-fashioned way using a pencil. Then the painting was done using a computer and some software called "Painter."

Have you drawn the pictures for lots of books? I've been an illustrator for ten years now so I've drawn a lot of pictures for books.

What do you like to draw most? Pigs, definitely pigs.

What gives you good ideas? Talking to other people gives me good ideas and makes me think.

Did you draw when you were a child? I drew all the time! I drew mainly spaceships and superheroes.

Will you try and write or draw a story too?

What did you like to do when you were a child? I liked reading, football, writing, and drawing. I hate football now though.

Can I be an illustrator like you? No, but you can be an illustrator like you!